I'm Lost, Duggy Dog!

Brian Ball

Illustrated by
Lesley Smith

Hamish Hamilton
London

For Emma

HAMISH HAMILTON LTD

Published by the Penguin Group
27 Wrights Lane, London W8 5TZ, England
Penguin Books USA Inc., 375 Hudson Street, New York, New York 10014, USA
Penguin Books Australia Ltd, Ringwood, Victoria, Australia
Penguin Books Canada Ltd, 10 Alcorn Avenue, Toronto, Ontario, Canada M4V 3B2
Penguin Books (NZ) Ltd, 182–190 Wairau Road, Auckland 10, New Zealand

Penguin Books Ltd, Registered Offices: Harmondsworth, Middlesex, England

First published in Great Britain 1989 by
Hamish Hamilton Children's Books

Copyright © 1989 by Sheila Lavelle
Illustrations copyright © 1989 by Paula Martyr
3 5 7 9 10 8 6 4 2

Printed in Hong Kong

A CIP catalogue record for this book is available from the British Library

ISBN 0-241-11990-1

Duggy Dog was snoozing under the bird-table in the garden.

Suddenly a large, fluffy head appeared over the garden wall.

It was a puppy. "Who are you?" she
said.

Duggy Dog opened one eye slowly.
"I'm Duggy Dog. And who are you?" he
asked.

"I'm Tina, and I'm lost, Duggy Dog,"
said the large, fluffy puppy.

Tina hopped over the garden wall. She
was a very large puppy indeed.

"Where are you lost from, Tina?"
asked Duggy Dog.

"I don't know," said Tina.

Duggy Dog wondered what to do.

Just then, Duggy thought he heard someone calling. It sounded like:
"Ti – na! Ti – na!"

"Who's calling?" said Duggy Dog.

Tina gave him a sly look. "I can't hear anyone calling," she said. And she rolled on to her back and made lost-little-puppy noises.

Duggy Dog felt sorry for Tina.

Suddenly Tina looked up and saw the bird-table.

The blackbirds were eating breakfast scraps.

"What's up there?" Tina said. "Food?"
Before Duggy could answer, she
reached up and ate every crumb.

Duggy Dog sighed. "You've eaten all
their breakfast," he said. "What am I
going to do with you?"

The big blackbird knew what to do.
"Send-her-back! Send-her-back where
she came from!" he squawked. And all
the blackbirds rushed at Tina with their
big, yellow beaks.

Tina yelped in fright. "Help me! I'm only a poor, lost puppy!" she cried, as the blackbirds chased her all the way down the garden.

Duggy Dog took Tina's collar. "Run!" he said.

Duggy Dog and Tina ran across the
Big Field to Floss's house.

Floss was in her garden. She was
minding the baby as he sat eating his
rusks.

"Hello," said Floss. "Who's your big,
fluffy friend?"

Duggy Dog explained that Tina was a poor, lost puppy. "Do you know where she lives?" he asked Floss.

But Floss had never seen Tina before, and she didn't know where she lived.

"Poor me," said Tina sadly. And she rolled on to her back and made lost-little-puppy noises.

Duggy Dog felt even more sorry for her.

Just then, Duggy thought he heard
someone calling. Again, it sounded like:
"Ti – na! Ti – na!"
Duggy Dog looked round for Tina.
Tina was by the pram. She was eating
the baby's rusks.
"TINA!" Duggy Dog cried.

"Waaa-waaa-waaa!" the baby cried.

"You're a very greedy lost puppy,
Tina!" said Floss. "Now see what you've
done!"

The baby's mother was coming down
the garden path. She had a cross look on
her face, and a large yard-brush in her
hands.

"Run!" cried Duggy Dog.

Floss didn't like the look of the yard-brush, either, so she ran too.

They dashed across the Big Field to Little Jasper's house.

Little Jasper wasn't in the garden, but his dinner was. And before Duggy Dog could stop her, Tina ate it all up.

Just then, Little Jasper came trotting
out of the house.

"Hello," he said. "Who's your big,
fluffy friend?"

Duggy Dog explained that Tina was a
poor, lost puppy. And that nobody knew
where she came from.

Little Jasper felt sorry for Tina. But
then he saw his empty dinner-bowl.

He looked at Duggy Dog.

He looked at Floss.

They shook their heads.

He looked at Tina. Tina opened her little black eyes as wide as they could go. She smiled sweetly.

"I was *ever* so hungry . . ." she said.

Little Jasper was very cross.

Duggy Dog sighed. Tina was a very naughty puppy. She had eaten the blackbirds' breakfast, and the baby's rusks, and now she had eaten Jasper's dinner. What *was* he going to do with her?

Duggy Dog sat down to think. At that
moment, Minty came running up.

"Hello, everyone. Have you seen a lost
puppy?"

"Yes!" they cried.

All eyes were on Tina.

"Oh good," said Minty, "because there's a girl in a blue dress and a red hat who's been calling a lost puppy called Tina for ages and ages. And Tina's dinner is ready."

"My dinner?" said Tina. "Sorry, I've got to go now. I'll see you all again next time I get lost."

And off she ran.

The others watched as the girl in the
blue dress gave Tina a big hug. Then
they saw Tina roll on to her back and
wave her paws in the air – just like a lost-
little-puppy.

Minty was glad that Tina wasn't lost
any more.

Jasper and Floss hoped that Tina
wouldn't get lost again . . .

"Hmm," said Duggy Dog. "I'm not
sure that Tina was ever really lost at all!"